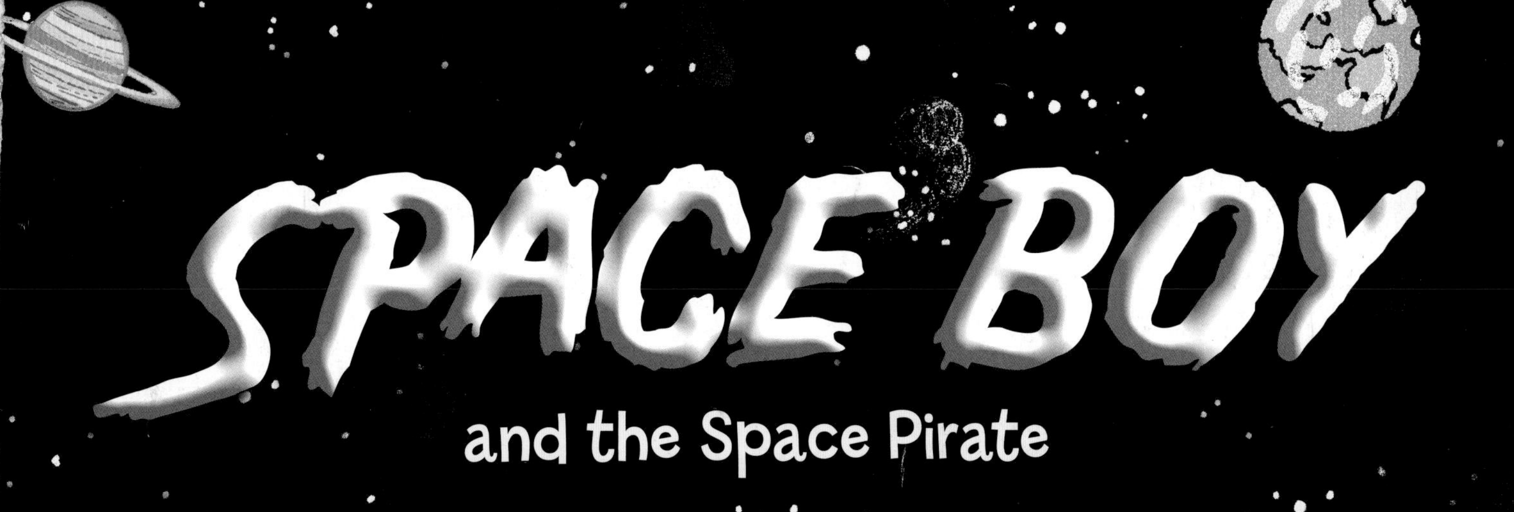

SPACE BOY

and the Space Pirate

Dian Curtis Regan

Illustrations by Robert Neubecker

Boyds Mills Press
An Imprint of Highlights
Honesdale, Pennsylvania

For Tyler and Andrew Palcer

—DCR

For Izzy and Jo

—RN

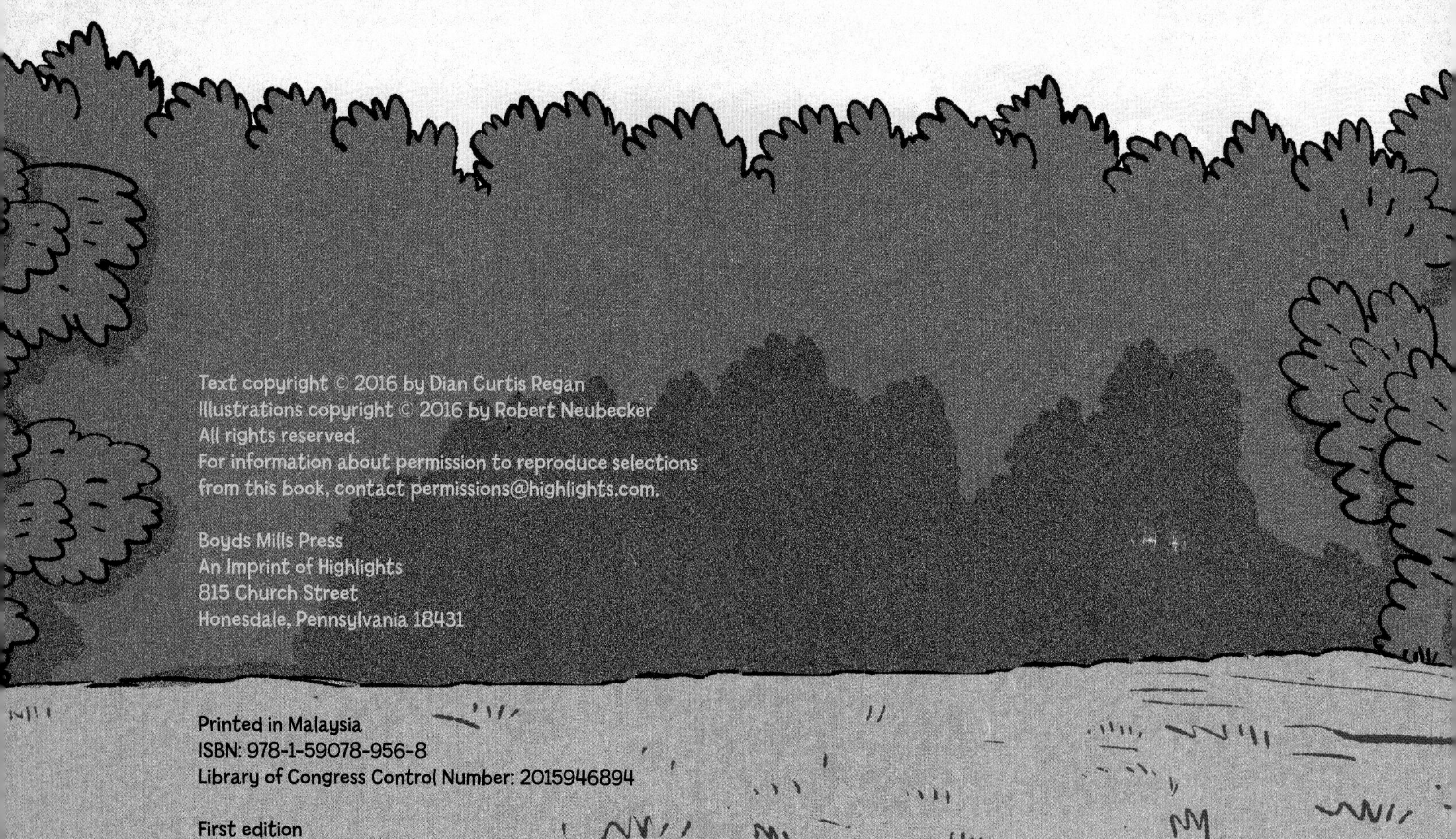

Boyds Mills Press
An Imprint of Highlights
815 Church Street
Honesdale, Pennsylvania 18431

Printed in Malaysia
ISBN: 978-1-59078-956-8
Library of Congress Control Number: 2015946894

First edition
The text of this book is set in Billy.
The illustrations are done digitally.
10 9 8 7 6 5 4 3 2 1

1. BEWARE!

Niko is reading a scary book
in the shade of his spaceship on Planet Home.

His copilot, Radar, and his dog, Tag, nap nearby.

"Pirates sneak aboard spaceships when the captain isn't looking," he reads.

Niko creeps aboard his spaceship to search the cargo hold—just in case.

He does not find any space pirates.

He searches the cockpit. No space pirates.

Niko opens the hatch to check outside. He spies his cousin, Sasha. Niko waves at her. "Come ride in my spaceship!"

Before Sasha can answer, someone yanks her away.

"Crew! Wake up!" calls Niko.
"A space pirate has kidnapped Sasha!"

Tag leaps awake, eager to chase . . . well, anythin
Radar is already on the case.

"They are headed toward Planet Zorg!" Niko cries.
"Board the spaceship, mates!
Prepare to blast off!"
NIKO
"Radar, are all systems *GO*?"
Radar checks all systems.
Tag prepares for blastoff.

2. PLANET ZORG!
VROO

The spaceship zips
between stars and lands
on Planet Zorg.

"Look!" says Niko.
"A clue! Fetch, Tag!"
Niko studies the scarf.
"Aha! These are pirate colors."
"Follow me!"

Captain and crew search the forests of Zorg.

"There they are!" Niko whispers.
"The space pirate is forcing Sasha to play with dolls!"
Radar thinks the space pirate looks a lot like Posh, Niko's sister.

Tag growls at the dolls.
They trigger bad memories.
Secretly, Radar thinks the dolls are cute.

3. The Captain's Plan

"Prepare for a surprise attack," Niko orders. "Stay low."

Captain and crew creep forward. Radar stays low.
He hopes no dolls will be harmed in the surprise attack.
Tag is not very good at creeping.
Or staying low.
Or attacking.
“We can see you,”
says the Posh pirate.

"Ahoy, Sasha! We have come to rescue you from the space pirate!"

"From the WHAT?" Sasha asks.

"Go away," orders Posh. "We do not want to be in your silly story."

"Sasha, stop playing with dolls! Come fly in my spaceship!"

"Come on, Sasha," the enemy says.
"Let's delete ourselves from this story."
"THE END!"

"It's MY story!" Niko calls after her. "I'll decide when to say 'THE END'!"

4. After Them!

Posh has thrown a twist into Niko's story!
Tag tugs on Niko's arm. The pirate and her captive are getting away!

“Noooooooo!” Niko cries. “The space pirate is stealing our ship!”

Tag does not like twists. He never knows which way to run.

Niko does not like being a captain without a ship.
"So, it's true," Niko says. "Pirates DO sneak aboard spaceships when the captain isn't looking."
His worried crew waits for orders.

"The space pirate has not defeated us," he tells them.
"A good captain always has a plan."
"Arf?"

"We must spacewalk back to Planet Home.
Follow me!"

5. Coming Home

Finally, Niko and his crew arrive on Planet Home.

The deleted space pirate and her maybe-captive are nowhere in sight.
BLAST
Niko searches his beloved spaceship.
Pirate booty!

"Crew!" Niko says. "We've been called to the Mother Ship.
Come, Tag. We must warn Mission Control about the mean space pirate."

forgot to end my story!”
“THE END!”
Meanwhile, back at the spaceship . . .

ZORG